Eddie Enough!

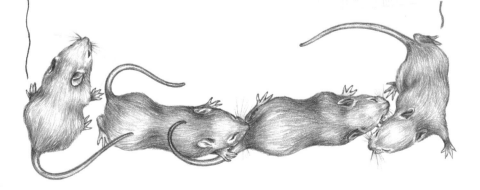

Library of Congress Cataloging in Publication Data

Zimmett, Debbie.
    Eddie Enough! / by Debbie Zimmett ; illustrated by Charlotte
Fremaux.—1st ed.
      p. cm.
    Summary: Third-grader Eddie Minetti is always getting in trouble at
school until his AD/HD is diagnosed and treated.
    ISBN 1-890627-25-9
    [Attention-deficit hyperactivity disorder—Fiction. 2. Schools—
Fiction.] I. Fremaux, Charlotte, ill. II. Title.

PZ7.Z638 Ed 2001
[E]—dc21
                                    2001017790

First Edition

10 9 8 7 6 5 4 3 2 1

Eddie Enough!

Written by Debbie Zimmett

Illustrated by Charlotte Murray Fremaux

WOODBINE HOUSE 2001

My name is Eddie. Actually my real name is Edward Anthony Minetti. The kids at school used to call me Eddie Spaghetti. I didn't really mind because we made weird rhymes out of everyone's name. For instance, we call my friend Neil "Banana Peel" and Jessica Leong is Jessica Ding-dong. So Eddie Spaghetti was okay.

Then one day the kids started calling me by a new name that actually doesn't rhyme with Eddie or Minetti. But first, I have to tell you about me.

I've always been in a hurry. Grandma says I was born running. I think she's kidding. I hop out of bed in the morning and jump down the stairs two at a time because I'm starving for breakfast! My dad says I eat like there's no tomorrow. I like to cook, too.

Some people say that I talk a lot. My mom tells me my first word actually was a sentence and I haven't stopped talking since. When Mom is annoyed with me, she says I even *listen* fast. I don't have any brothers and sisters. But that's okay because Dad says I fill up the house all by myself!

I'm in third grade. Our class doesn't have real desks. I'm lucky because my table partner, Rachel, is usually too busy doing her work to complain that I jiggle my leg. Sometimes I bump her elbow but it's always an accident. I can't help it if I'm a lefty!

My favorite subject is Math. I try not to call out but I get excited when I know the answer! My teacher, Mrs. Pinck, says I have to give the others a chance to show that they know the answers, too. You know what's really weird? Sometimes Mrs. Pinck *does* call on me and I don't hear her right away.

So that's how things were. But a few weeks ago, my life, like Grandpa says, went from bad to worse. At breakfast, I spilled orange juice on Dad's new suit when I was sliding into home plate. Actually, I mean into the kitchen. Then, halfway to school, I remembered that I forgot my lunch.

Even though I ran all the way, I got to school after my class started the spelling test. I missed the first three words so I looked at Rachel's paper. Miss Perfect Rachel told Mrs. Pinck that I was cheating. Honestly, I wasn't! I just wanted to see what words I missed. Mrs. Pinck made me sit next to Neil, who made a big deal about covering up his paper.

It was my turn to collect the test papers and when I put them on Mrs. Pinck's desk, her husband fell over. Actually, her husband didn't fall over but his picture did, which knocked Andrew's jar of sea monkeys to the floor. By the way, Andrew didn't know that sea monkeys actually aren't monkeys at all but a kind of tiny shrimp. And they sure are hard to scoop up off the floor.

I figured that Tiny, our class rat, would be able to clean up the sea monkeys really fast. I was right. But then Jessica almost stepped on Tiny, so I had to yell, "STOP" really loud.

Tiny got scared and ran under the sink. That was when Mrs. Pinck said, "I've had enough, Eddie, enough!"

The whole class thought it was funny. Neil yelled, "Eddie Enough, Eddie Enough," like that's my name. Then some of the other kids said it, too. I pushed Neil and he stepped on Jessica's toe and she started to cry.

Mrs. Pinck sent me out into the hallway. She told me I needed to slow down. It's weird because that's what Mom always says. The hallway was quiet and kind of dark. Maybe that's what makes kids slow down. The principal, Mr. Thomas, walked by, but he just smiled. Maybe he was slowing down, too.

After awhile, Mrs. Pinck stuck her head out of the classroom and I must have looked slower because she told me I could join the class for library.

I hate library time because we have to pick out chapter books. Chapter books have too many words! I lay on the carpet. Mrs. Pinck walked over and said very quietly, "Eddie, you have thirty seconds to choose a book and start reading." She didn't say "or else," but it sure sounded that way.

I pulled a book off the shelf. Great! It was boring nonfiction! I was going to put it back, but Mrs. Pinck was still watching me. So I opened the book and began to read. It actually wasn't a bad book. It was about a

man who rescues wild animals. It sounded like a cool job. Until I read, "injured animals must be approached slowly and quietly or they may become fearful and try to attack." I closed the book. I guess that's not a job for me! Good thing Pinkie wasn't watching while I put the book away.

Neil was holding two books on baseball. I figured he didn't need them both so I took one. Nobody heard him complain because the lunch bell started to ring.

Lunch is usually my favorite subject, but not that day! As soon as I got to the lunch room, Neil started singing, "Eddie Enough thinks he's tough!" It didn't take long before the entire table joined in. Even Vladimir, who doesn't speak English, was trying to say the words. I felt like I got punched in the stomach. So I smashed Vladimir's banana.

The lunchroom aide sent me to the office to eat my lunch. Mr. Thomas saw me. It's pretty cool the way he can raise one eyebrow. I tried to do it but my mouth kept curling up.

After lunch, we had art. Mr. Starr set a famous portrait on an easel. A portrait is where a person sits very still for a long time while the artist paints his picture.

Mr. Starr told us to "buddy up" and draw each other's portrait. In one second, everyone had a partner except me and Shelley Sue. I don't like Shelley because she's bossy, but the way things were going I figured I'd better be nice. That is, until Shelley said, "But Mr. Starr, I can't draw Eddie because he never sits still!" Everyone laughed. Before I knew it, I pinched her arm and called her Smelly Shelley.

Mr. Starr sent me out into the hall to cool off. "It won't work," I told him. "Mrs. Pinck already tried that."

I didn't mean to knock over the easel. And I honestly tried to catch the colored chalk before it spilled. Did you know that chalk makes weird crunching noises when you step on it? That's when Mr. Starr decided that I needed to go to the office.

I was pretty mad, so when the door closed behind me it sounded mad, too. Mr. Starr made me come back and go out again "quietly." This time the door sounded fine but my feet were angry. The third time, my feet behaved but I bumped my head on the door because my eyes were all hot and blurry. I could hear the kids laughing even after I carefully shut the door.

Handyman Joe had just mopped the floor and there were yellow signs, CAUTION! SLIPPERY WHEN WET, standing in the hallway. I kicked them over, took a big running start, and slid along the wet floor.

How was I supposed to know that Mr. Thomas was coming around the corner? He had this look on his face that told me I'd better go back and set up those yellow signs. Then we went into his office for a "chat." Did you know that he could have a soda anytime he wants? But actually, he uses his refrigerator for healthy stuff like juice. I had cranberry.

"Bad day?" asked Mr. Thomas.

"It's the worst day of my life!" I told Mr. Thomas about Dad's orange juice and the sea monkeys and scaring Tiny and the colored chalk. "But the worst thing is that all the kids call me Eddie Enough! Pretty soon they'll call me Eddie Too Much."

It's a good thing Mr. Thomas didn't have carpet in his office because the cranberry juice that I spilled could leave an awful stain. It was an accident! After we cleaned up the juice, Mr. Thomas said that some kids can't help being "too much."

Then he told me something else. Mr. Thomas said that when he was in third grade, he was a lot like me. Mr. Thomas? Like me? I could hardly believe it!

Mr. Thomas had a conference with my parents. My parents told Mr. Thomas that I was too bouncy at home, too.

Well, to make a long story longer, as Grandma would say, first my mom made an appointment for me to get a checkup. She and my dad wanted to make sure I wasn't sick.

They couldn't promise that I wouldn't get a shot, so I was really happy when the nurse said I wouldn't need one! The nurse weighed and measured me. She checked my hearing and my vision, too. The doctor listened to my heart and lungs. He said that I am a perfect specimen. Whatever that means.

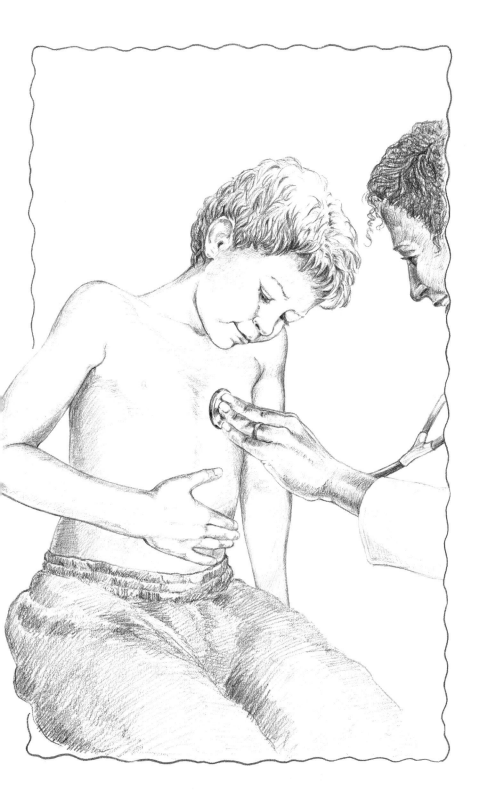

Soon after that I was excused from class a couple of times to take some special tests with a lady named Dr. Joan. The tests weren't much different than the ones we have in school. One time, I looked at pictures and we talked about them. Another time, I read stories and answered questions about what I read. We also did these really neat math puzzles. After every test, Dr. Joan let me pick a prize from her treasure chest.

I got a book of riddles: "What is the longest word in the English language?" The answer is, "smiles, because there's a mile between the first and last letters." That's my favorite because Neil didn't get it!

When my friends asked me why I got to leave the classroom, I told them it's because I'm special. And that's not a lie because Dad says everybody is special in one way or another.

Finally, it was time for everyone to put all the pieces of the puzzle together. The good news is I'm pretty smart. But, I need to stop bouncing and pay attention.

The doctor gave my parents a prescription for special medicine to help me look before I leap, as Grandpa would say. I go to the health office every day before lunch to take my medicine. Some of the kids ask why I always have to go see the nurse. I tell them I take medicine.

Did you know that everybody takes medicine sometimes? I hope there is a pill for Smelly Shelley.

One day, Dr. Joan visited my class. She taught everybody a good way to stay out of trouble. It's called S.T.A.R. or STOP, THINK, ACT, and REVIEW. Dr. Joan said when we S.T.A.R, we make better choices and learn from our mistakes.

Did you know that everyone has to S.T.A.R. sometimes? Even Miss Perfect Rachel! And guess what? S.T.A.R. works on grownups, too.

I still visit Dr. Joan once in awhile. She asks me about my day and while we talk I draw or make things out of clay. She showed me and my mom how to make a sticker chart to help me remember my lunch. If I remember for a whole week, I get a dollar.

You know what's better than the dollar? It's knowing that everyone wants to help me do better. But don't tell my mom because I like the dollar, too.

Speaking of lunch, Neil opened his lunch one day to find that his tuna sandwich was missing. All that was left was the plastic wrap. Of course, Neil blamed me because I used to always forget my lunch. But I'm remembering my lunch and anyway I hate tuna.

Later on, Shelley heard lots of little squeaks coming from under the cubbies. Handyman Joe moved the cubbies and there was Tiny with six new babies. Mrs. Pinck said, "I guess that's where the tuna fish sandwich disappeared."

Then guess what? Mrs. Pinck let me scoop up the babies and put them in the cage with Tiny. I remembered the library book and moved the babies slowly and quietly so Tiny wouldn't worry.

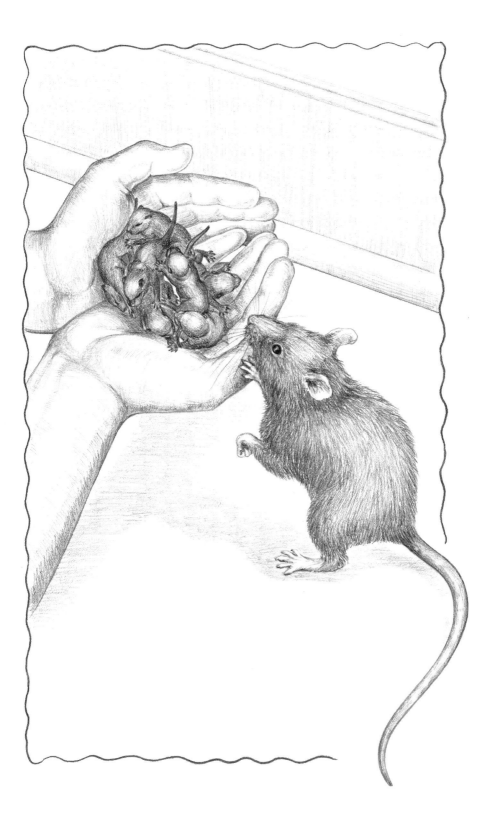

The best part of all is that I'm not Eddie Enough anymore. And deep down inside, I actually feel like Eddie Just Right!

Why I Wrote this Story...

Hi, this is Eddie again. If you are reading this book, there's a good chance that you or someone you know has Attention-Deficit/ Hyperactivity Disorder. That's quite a mouthful, so most people call it AD/HD for short.

So what do all those initials mean, anyway? My mom and dad explained it to me this way: Some kids have a hard time paying attention in school. They start out listening to what their teacher is saying, but end up staring out the window at a falling leaf, listening to the grinding noise of the pencil sharpener, or smelling something yummy coming from the cafeteria and dreaming about lunch! Other kids act

"bouncy." That's my family's way of describing me when I'm crashing into things and fidgety.

Don't let people tell you that people with AD/HD are stupid. Actually, many kids and grownups who have AD/HD are quite creative and smart. The reason we might not do as well in school or at work is because it's hard to learn when you can't sit still or pay attention.

I want you to know that if you have AD/HD, you are not alone. At least three kids out of every hundred have it, too! And the great news is that there are many people, like your parents, teachers, doctors, and therapists, who want to help you be the best you can be.

About the Author

Debbie Zimmett is an instructional assistant and Applied Behavior Analysis therapist for preschool students with special needs in the Las Virgenes Unified School District in Southern California. After earning a baccalaureate degree in nursing from University of Pennsylvania, she worked in various hospital and public health settings until her current position. She lives with her family in Calabasas, California.

About the Illustrator

Charlotte Fremaux has been drawing ever since she could hold a pencil. Although her major in college was art history, working in the studio was her love, and she eventually surrendered to her fate. She has worked as a fine artist, graphic designer and illustrator, and finds illustrating for children the best of all worlds. She was born in New Orleans, left her heart in Hawaii, and currently lives in the Maryland suburbs of Washington, D.C., with her husband and son, who, at eleven, is already preparing to follow his mother in her chosen field.